## DATE DUE

| | |
|---|---|
| OCT - 4 2001 | |
| OCT 27 2001 | |
| AUG 28 2002 | |
| | |
| OCT - 4 2002 | |
| NOV 14 2002 | |
| | |
| | |
| | |
| | |
| | |
| | |
| | |
| | |

DEMCO, INC. 38-2931

# BEST WITCHES

## POEMS FOR HALLOWEEN

by Jane Yolen / illustrated by Elise Primavera

G. P. Putnam's Sons    New York

To my favorite ghosts,
*Will & Isabelle Yolen*
JY

To my teacher,
*Jack Henderson*
E P

# CONTENTS

## THE MAGIC HOUSE

We should have known when we tasted the eaves,
Breaking them off like toffee
And cramming them into our mouths.
And the dear little windows, the color of coffee,
And chocolate doorknobs,
And windowpanes striped with mint.
We should have guessed at the chimney smoke,
White marshmallow fluff.
Taken the hint
From the marzipan bricks
And the fenceposts made of bone rubble.
But it was only when we saw the witch
That we knew we were in deep, deep trouble.

## WITCH PIZZA

No anchovies,
Lots of cheese,
Amanita
Mushrooms, please.

Top with herbs
Both hot and chivey,
And some extra
Poison ivy.

# KNOCK, KNOCK

I'm a specter, I'm a spirit,
I'm a revenant, a shade,
I'm a disembodied being
And the fiercest ever made.

*Go away,
I see your feet.
You're just Diane
In a white bed sheet.*

I'm a phantom, I'm a shadow,
I'm a vision, I'm a haunt,
I'm an insubstantial presence.
It's your blood I really want.

Go away,
I see your feet.
You're just Marie
In a white bed sheet.

I'm a banshee, I'm an aura,
I'm a grave shape, I'm a ghost,
I'm an ectoplasmic sighting
And I'd like some tea and toast.

Go away . . . oh, no,
My gosh, it's true!
I'm getting out of here. . . .

BOO!
HOO!

## SPELLS

I need no spell to get me through
A tangled fence of briars.
I need no spell to help me pass
A wall of burning fires.

I need no spell to make a dress
Of silk from one of chintz.
I need no spell to turn a frog
Into a handsome prince.

But if you've got a spell around
That gets my homework right,
Or one that makes my mother think
I've gone to bed at night,

Or one that takes the garbage out,
Or one that feeds the cat,
I'd pay you my allowance
If you had a spell like that!

## HOW TO SPELL
(A Jump Rope Rhyme)

Cross your fingers, cross your eyes,
Touch your tongue to nose.
Turn three times with creature cries,
That's how a good spell goes.

Mutter things that start with X,
Turn widdershins about.
Cross your heart and hold your breath,
For O-U-T spells OUT!

# SILLY QUESTIONS

For the witch's tv show
Here are things you have to know
If you want to win a prize.
Are you Halloweeny wise?

*What is a witch with poison ivy called?*
AN ITCHY WITCHY. (Yukka-yukka-yukka!)

For the witch's tv show
Here are things you have to know
If you want to win a prize.
Are you Halloweeny wise?

*Who does a ghoul fall in love with?*
HIS GHOUL FRIEND. (Yukka-yukka-yukka!)

For the witch's tv show
Here are things you have to know
If you want to win a prize.
Are you Halloweeny wise?

*Where do vampires live?*
IN THE VAMPIRE STATE BUILDING. (Yukka-yukka-yukka!)

For the witch's tv show
Here are things you have to know
If you want to win a prize.
Are you Halloweeny wise?

*Who are some of the werewolf's cousins?*
THE WHAT WOLVES AND THE WHEN WOLVES. (Yukka-yukka-yukka!)

All my questioning is through,
Now the rest is up to you.
You have passed the witch's test.
Now *you* must make up the rest!

# THE FOSSILOT

You cannot find a Fossilot
Except in ancient stones,
Where imprints of its teeth and claws
Lie jumbled with its bones.

Some scientists cleaned up the bones,
Arranged, then tried to date them.
But when they had the jaw complete —
It turned around and ate them.

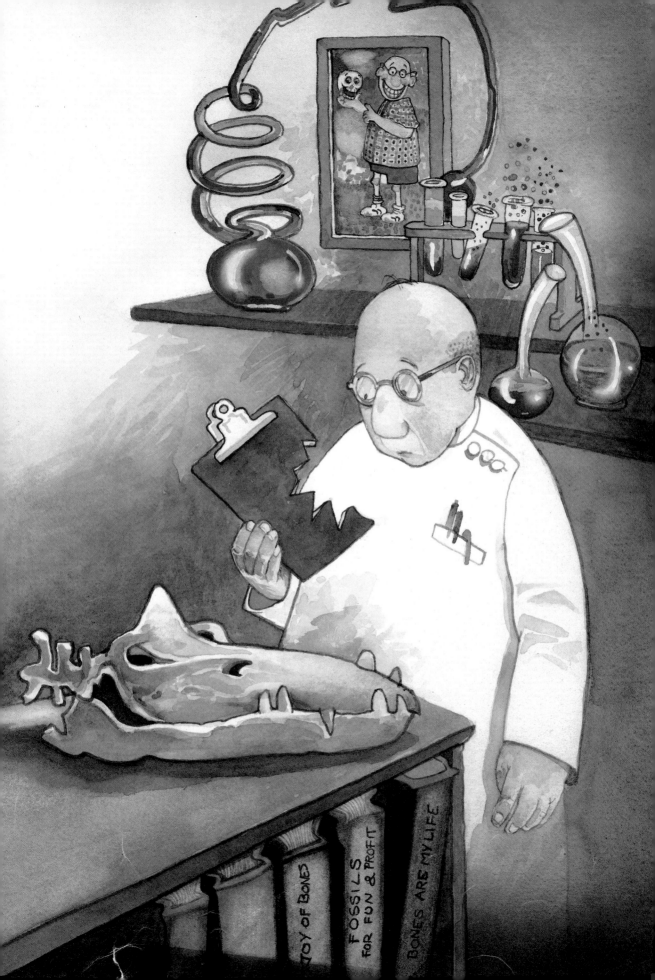

## THE OLD MAN OF THE WOOD

I went into the willow-wood
To strip a branching bare,
And spied an old man by a stream
With leaves in place of hair.

His fingers were like thorny twigs,
His knuckles knobs of bone,
His legs were gray and heavy
As if carven out of stone.

His face was seamed with jagged lines
And crusted hard as bark,
His voice was whispery like the wind
That haunts the woods at dark.

He said but this one thing to me
That long I've pondered on:
"Your kind is like the yearwood,
Quickly harvested, then gone."

# LETTER FROM A WITCH NAMED FLO

Dear Sirs:
  The broom I purchased at
Your store today, and the black hat
(Size 6½) are quite a mess
And neither of them match my dress.
My dress is black, so I can't see
How difficult a match could be,
Just basic black, no patterned swirls,
No curlicues, no fancy whirls,
No crosses, checks or polkadots,
Just midnight black — and lots and lots
Of cobwebs all around the hem.
Your salesgirl promised, "No problem.
At Halloween we sell a ton,
And never have returns — not one!"
  Well, I'm returning hat and broom.
I won't be caught dead in a tomb
In either of these items.
      So . . .

Send back my check.

     Best witches,

       *Flo*

## SONG OF THE MODERN WITCH

Oh, I'm the model of a major modern witch,
No more spiky hats and mangy cats for me.
You will see me dining grandly at the Ritz,
Having chocolate mousse and croissants with my tea.

No more forest huts and messy pots and such,
And no more icy midnight rides upon a broom.
You will find me in my condominium
Cleaning up with my electrical vacuum!

## ADVICE ON HOW TO SLEEP WELL
## HALLOWEEN NIGHT

The thing to remember when you go to bed
Is hang strings of garlic high over your head,
So werewolves and vampires won't come to call.
In fact you won't get many callers at all
'Cause garlic is smelly, besides its success
With magical creatures who visit distress
On humans who read scarey stories at night,
And sleep in their bedrooms without a night-light.

The thing to remember when you go to bed
Is putting a cross at your foot and your head,
'Cause witches and vampire bats are religious
And touching a sign like a cross gives them hidjous
Goosebumps and warts, hives, the welts and the itches,
Which *nobody* likes, even v. bats and witches.
But try not to toss or to turn in your bed.
If you kick off the crosses you're gonna wake dead.

The thing to remember when you go to bed
Is watch out for goblins who munch on your head.
What stops them is water, so ask for a glass,
Then pour it around so the goblins can't pass.
Or else make a run for the bathroom and turn
On the hot and cold faucets and watch goblins squirm.
As a last chance, since goblins all fear running streams,
If you don't own a bathroom, dream water-filled dreams.

So—that's my advice. Now just turn off the light.
Hope you sleep well the next Halloween night!

# THE USED-CARPET SALESMAN

And here's a carpet, slightly torn,
Lovely pattern, hardly worn.
A little fraying on the sides,
But well equipped for long, smooth rides.
A brand new horn and brand new shocks.
It comes with silver packing box.
Extras? Seat belts, radio,
This baby is all set to go.
Luxurious—and ample room.
Trade in your car—or else your broom.
The price is low. And I'll take checks.
Sign on the line.
                    And thank *you*.
                              NEXT!

$199.99

## AT THE WITCH'S DRUGSTORE

Camel's oil.
Camomile.
Dragon's blood.
Dramamine.
Adder's tongue.
Adhesive tape.
Phoenix feathers.
Phenobarb.
Eye of newt.
Iodine.
Asp venom.
Aspirin.

Just take two
And call the witch doctor
in the morning.

# THE GRAMMATICAL WITCH

The other day I saw a witch,
Or maybe it was two,
Though teacher says my grammar's wrong
And that I saw a *who*.

Now I can't spell as witches can;
My grammar's often weak.
And teacher has to show me how
To write the words I speak.

And I can't count too awfully well,
And whether one or more
I can't be sure — as witches go —
She wasn't three or four.

And *who* my witch was I don't know,
Yet there's one thing I do:
I know that she was sure a witch
Which proves she's not a who.

# MAGIC WANDS

When I was young I had a wand
of willow.
It was yellow
and could bend.
My spells were several
and rather callow.
I lent my willow
to a friend.

When I was older my wand
was cedar,
the color of cider
and very strong.
My spells were many
(though the meter
didn't matter)
and much too long.

And now I have a wand
of oaken,
more a token
of my mind.
My spells are few and
oft unspoken,
lest I'm mistaken
or unkind.

I've found that magic
of any measure
can bring one pleasure
or much pain.
The wand's a symbol
of a treasure.
It's heart — not hand —
one has to train.

# IVY

Mirrored in the window pane
Slivers of moon creep past the glass,
Scaling the side of my oak-brown desk,
Stabbing at objects as they pass.
Reaching the door, they wither and fall
While ivy is climbing the redbrick wall.

Softly a scratching outside of the room,
A scraping, a creeping, a hesitant crawl
Sounds far below the window sill
For ivy is climbing the redbrick wall.
I wait, cold, in the still of my bed.
The ivy will cover me when I am dead.

## TOMBMATES

I am a tidy sort of ghost,
But *she* likes clutter, muss, and mess.
I wear a clean and ironed shirt.
*She* wears a rags-and-tatters dress.
I never leave my chains around
But hang them up when not in use.
*She* leaves hers lying anywhere,
And heaps upon me such abuse.
She calls me "White eyes," "Booger Ben,"
She calls me "Mausoleum Breath."
I tell you, she has really made
It hard to come to terms with death.
Do you think that there might be
A single in Eternity?

# THE WARLOCK'S CAT

A shadow of a shadow
Slipping in and out of night,
With his claws and teeth like starshine
Flickering on the edge of sight.

He is blacker than a night wind,
He is darker than a coal,
For he's the outward casting
Of his fearsome master's soul.

## ALONE ON A BROOM

The sky surrounds me,
Jupiter crowns me,
The moon rides on my back.

The wind sings to me,
The night rings through me
As I fly down the track.

The trees zip past me,
The stars all cast me
In silver shadows and light.

I'll never do better,
Whatever the weather,
Than riding on Halloween night.

## THE WITCH'S CAULDRON

Round as a pot,
Deep as a spell,
Dark as a midnight,
Cold as a well,
Strong as a wish,
Hard as a hate,
Full as a moon,
Brutal as fate.

# DO WITCHES HAVE?

Do witches have babies?
  No, witches have toads.
  They find them in wellsprings
  Or on country roads.

Do witches have babies?
  No, witches have cats
  Who sleep amongst broomstraws
  Or curl up in hats.

Do witches have babies?
  No, witches have snakes
  That twine around broomsticks
  Or vampire stakes.

Do witches have babies?
  Of course witches do.
  If we don't have babies —
  Then how come there's you?

ACKNOWLEDGMENTS

"The Old Man of the Wood," copyright © 1984 by Jane Yolen, first appeared in
*Fantasy and Terror #2*, edited by Jessica Amanda Salmonson.
"The Fossilot," copyright © 1980 by Jane Yolen, first appeared in
*Isaac Asimov's Science Fiction Magazine.*

Text copyright © 1989 by Jane Yolen. Illustrations copyright © 1989 by Elise Primavera.
All rights reserved. This book, or parts thereof, may not be reproduced in any form without permission in
writing from the publisher. Published simultaneously in Canada
Printed in Hong Kong by South China Printing Co. (1988) Ltd.
Book design by Charlotte Staub. Lettering by David Gatti.

Library of Congress Cataloging-in-Publication Data
Yolen, Jane.   Best witches.
Summary: The author presents her own poetry on witches,
ghosts, magic, and other aspects of Halloween.
I. Halloween — Juvenile poetry.   2. Witchcraft — Juvenile poetry.
3. Children's poetry, American.   [I. Witches — Poetry.
2. Halloween — Poetry.   3. American poetry]
I. Primavera, Elise, ill.   II. Title.
PS3575.043B47   1988   811'.54   88-5866
ISBN 0-399-21539-5
3   5   7   9   10   8   6   4